D1513381

What any author wants is for his books to become dog-eared and familiar. I've been lucky enough that my very young readers are particularly adept at giving their books doggy ears in no time at all.

And of all my books, perhaps it's those about Kipper that get the doggiest ears of all, which I guess is kind of appropriate.

Mick Inkpen

First published in 2002
by Hodder Children's Books

This edition published in 2016 by Hodder and Stoughton

Text and illustrations copyright © Mick Inkpen 2002

Hodder Children's Books
An imprint of
Hachette Children's Group
Part of Hodder and Stoughton
Carmelite House
50 Victoria Embankment
London EC4Y 0DZ

ISBN: 978 1 444 93702 2

Printed in China

An Hachette UK Company
www.hachette.co.uk

Kipper's Monster

Mick Inkpen

Hodder
Children's
Books

Tiger had a brand new torch.
'It's the most powerful torch there is!' he said to Kipper.
He shone it at Big Owl.
He shone it at Hippo.
He shone it in Kipper's face.
'You should see it when it's dark!' he said. 'It's REALLY good when it's dark!'

He sat in Kipper's basket
and pulled the blanket over
his head.

'Come on! We can make it dark
under here!' he said.

Under the blanket was one of
Kipper's storybooks.

'That's another thing!' said Tiger.
'You can read under the bedclothes
with a torch like this!'

Kipper began to read.
'Deep in the middle of the
dark, dark wood, there lived a horrible,
horrendous, terrible, tremendous. . .'

'That's it!' shouted Tiger, jumping up.
'We'll camp in the woods tonight!
It'll be really, REALLY dark in
the woods.'

'Shall I bring my
book?' said Kipper.

So they took the book and
some biscuits and they put up
their tent in the middle of the woods,
at the bottom of Big Hill.

But as it began to get dark
Tiger began to think that perhaps
it wasn't such a good idea after all.

'Come inside and have a
biscuit,' said Kipper. 'Do you
want Rabbit or
Big Owl?'

But Tiger didn't reply. He was looking nervously out of the door. 'Do you think there are any bears in these woods?' he whispered.

'No, I shouldn't think so,' said Kipper. He began to read.

'Deep in the middle of the dark, dark wood, there lived a horrible...'

But Tiger wasn't ready. He asked Kipper to sit next to the door, instead of him. And when Kipper tried again to read, Tiger got up and zipped the door shut altogether.

But the third time Kipper tried to read, from somewhere outside the tent, there came the most terrible, tremendous, horrible, horrendous,

'Screech!'

'What was that?' said Kipper.
Tiger said nothing.

'Let's go and look!' whispered
Kipper. So they crept out of the tent
and into the woods, shining Tiger's
torch ahead of them.

'I think it came from somewhere
near here,' said Kipper. The torch
beam lit up the enormous, grey
trunk of an old tree.

There in the middle was
a dark, dark hole.

Suddenly a huge pair of
yellow eyes blinked open, and
from the hole came the most terrible,

'Screech!'

They shrieked and ran, bumping
into each other and sending the
torch flying. They scrambled into the
tent and lay there panting hard,
listening. . .

'I think it was just an owl,' whispered Kipper. 'Yes, it was just a silly, old owl.'

But behind him, the shadow of something was growing on the wall of the tent.

Something with horns.

'It's a horrible, horrendous monster!' squealed Tiger.
The shape on the tent grew and grew till it was looming above them.

Then slowly it changed into a shape that Kipper had seen before.

Kipper crept out of the tent and walked towards the torchlight. There, caught in the beam, was a little snail.

Kipper picked up the torch and let the snail crawl on to his paw. He looked at the snail closely.

Its horns curled in and out as he touched them.

'I've found the horrible,
horrendous monster!
Look Tiger!'
Tiger peeped out from
underneath the blanket.
He saw the snail.
He saw its shadow.
He felt silly.

'Shall I read the story now?'
said Kipper.

But Kipper never did get to read his story, because they went home to Tiger's house, where they put up the tent in Tiger's bedroom. . .

. . .and Tiger got to read it instead.